A Secret Place

Scholastic Children's Books
Scholastic Publications Ltd
7-9 Pratt Street, London NW1 0AE, UK

Scholastic Inc
730 Broadway, New York, NY 10003, USA

Scholastic Canada Ltd
123 Newkirk Road, Richmond Hill, Ontario, Canada L4C 3G5

Ashton Scholastic Pty Ltd
PO Box 579, Gosford, New South Wales, Australia

Ashton Scholastic Ltd
Private Bag 1, Penrose, Auckland, New Zealand

First published by Scholastic Publications Ltd, 1992
This edition published, 1993

Copyright © Julia Draper, 1992

ISBN 0 590 55270 8

Printed by Proost International Book Production

10 9 8 7 6 5 4 3 2 1

A Secret Place

Hippo

When we moved into our house, the garden was a
mess. I found an empty paint can, an old pair of boots
and even a bashed up kettle.

Across the road there was a big patch of waste ground, just like a jungle.

It was my special, secret place.

The thistles were nearly as tall as me. On some nights I thought I could hear a fox.

I always saw the same spotty butterfly on the purple, spiky flowers. Birds came to eat the squashy berries, insects and worms.

One day men in hard hats came.

The next time I looked for my
favourite butterfly they sent me away.

Then they dug up my secret place and burned the spiky flowers.

The animals disappeared. They must have been scared
of the machines.

Mum said the men were going to build new flats, so maybe Gran would have a place of her own at last.

Every night when the builders had gone, I listened for the fox, but it never came.

Then I had an idea. I thought I would try and get the animals and insects to come back.

First, I asked Dad to help me clear our garden.

Some of the rubbish looked useful so I
kept it.

I got some books from the library about how animals and plants live together.

Mum took me to market and we chose
lots of seeds. We also bought some bags of
soil because ours was so stony.

As soon as we got home, I tipped out some of the seeds. Would they ever look like the pictures on the packets?

I used an old washing-up bowl to make a little pool for frogs, and put in rocks and bricks to give them a dark place to hide.

Mum showed me how to nail one of
the boots to a post. She said maybe a
robin would nest in it.

I left some old planks and dry leaves in a corner for insects, and perhaps even a hedgehog. I left the other boot for a mouse or a toad to nest in.

I put the seeds in the things I had saved when we cleared the garden. I left them in the sun and watered them often.

I waited and watched...

As the leaves began to show, I noticed more and more insects. Then the birds came back.

At last I saw the butterfly
with the spots. One night I'm
sure I heard the fox.

I had my own special, secret place again.